To the Handlers: Daniel, Lisa & Otto—
expert practitioners of the summertime nap

Text and illustrations copyright © 2015 by Mo Willems

Library of Congress Cataloging-in-Publication Data

Willems, Mo, author, illustrator.
I will take a nap! / by Mo Willems.
pages cm
"An Elephant & Piggie Book."
Summary: Gerald is tired and cranky and wants to take a nap, but Piggie is not helping.
ISBN 978-1-4847-1630-4
[1. Naps (Sleep) —Fiction. 2. Elephants—Fiction. 3. Pigs—Fiction. 4. Friendship—Fiction.] I. Title.
PZ7.W65535Ib 2015
[E]—dc23   2014040522

Visit www.hyperionbooksforchildren.com and www.pigeonpresents.com

First Edition, June 2015
10 9 8 7 6 5 4 3 2 1
F850-6835-5-15046

Printed in Singapore
Reinforced binding

An ELEPHANT & PIGGIE Book

Hyperion Books for Children
New York

AN IMPRINT OF DISNEY BOOK GROUP

I Will Take a Nap!

By **Mo Willems**

And cranky.

I like to nap.

I am happier
when I am rested.

7

11

12

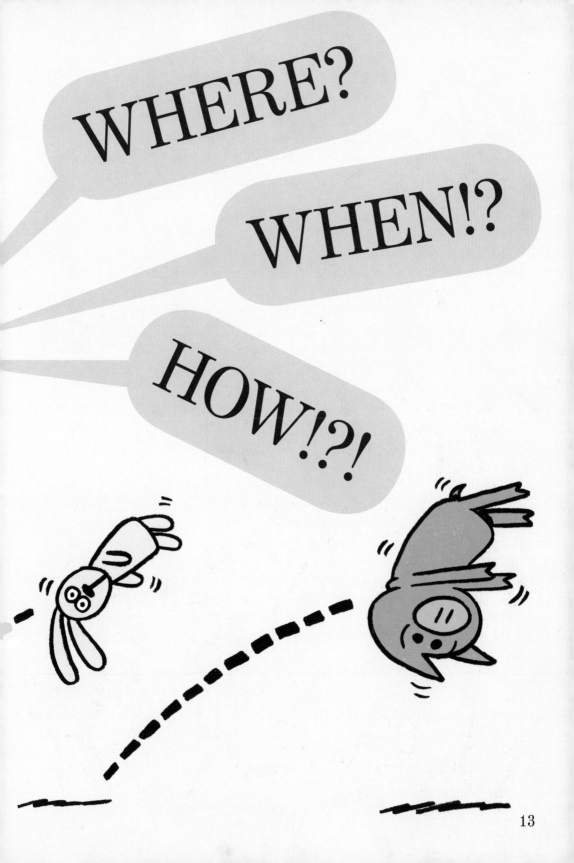

14

15

17

18

21

25

28

29

35

36

37

39

41

44

47

51

52

53

I sure did, *Turnip Head.*

Elephant and Piggie have more funny adventures in: